SHISHIRA

ASHIRA

Made with ♥ on the Notion Press Platform
www.notionpress.com

I dedicate this book to my family, friends and well-wishers for their support and guidance. This wouldn't be possible without you all.

Contents

FOREWORD

From the moment I began writing this book until it was finally published, I have learned and experienced countless things. This is not just a book; it is a dream I once had, a dream I could never forget and made me write about it.

I never thought I would write a book someday. I was never a writer or dreamt of writing a book. But this book is something special to me. I had this story but no confidence to put it on paper. And there comes, my friends and family. The motivation they gave woke up the writer in me. I am grateful to them for motivating me to write it.

My journey with this book made an incredible mark in my life. I hope you too will like this journey with this book filled with fantasy, thrill and mystery.

ACKNOWLEDGEMENTS

This is my first book. Writing this book wasn't a piece of cake. I am grateful to all the people for all the support they provided.

Firstly, Amma and Appa, you guys are the best! I love you so much. You guys are a mixture of cool and strict parents. But your encouragement made me the person I am today. And my brother, I know you never read my book properly. Take this as a reminder and read it.

And then my friends. I know I irritated you all by making you listen to my story, read my script and give reviews almost 100 times. Thanks for tolerating me and giving me your suggestions on improving my story. This book exists because of you guys.

Lastly, thanks to you - yes, the one holding this book. I am happy that my book caught your eye. I hope you love this book and enjoy reading it.

I

THE DREAM

Long, long ago, in the vast lands of India, during the era where the jewels on the street appeared like colourful illumination lights, the air with the fragrance of Sandalwood and exquisite flowers, there was a Dravida *Kingdom Shankarachala* ruled by *King Chakra*. The Kingdom was well known not only for its Invincible troops but also for its astonishing ways of exorcism. It was one of the wealthiest kingdoms with Great Literates.

Far towards the west was the peaceful Kingdom of Albada, filled with abundant knowledge and advanced technologies. It was ruled by the virtuous *Queen Cynthia*, known for her breathtaking beauty and phenomenal battle skills. Even a Queen like her faced some trouble, the trouble that made a peaceful Kingdom like Albada Hell.

Cynthia was one of the King Chakra's closest acquaintances. One day she decided to visit him, out of nowhere. She sent a messenger to the King Chakra about her visit but didn't specify the reason.

The Queen then took her strong men, left the kingdom to her brother, and set sail to Shankarachala. She didn't want to go empty-handed, thus she brought Diamonds, Jewels and innumerable gifts in which one dark maroon box which had ancient symbols imprinted on it looked suspicious. It was kept in a corner of the ship, separately from all the other gifts, which only Queen had the access to.

The morning was filled with the pleasant smell of the ocean. The cry of the dolphins was harmonising with the song of the Seagles making it a wake-up song for the Queen. It's already been a week since they set sail. The Queen came out with a fresh face which turned into excitement when she encountered a beach with fishermen preparing the nets, cloths set to dry on the rope and kids playing Tag.

"Ah! We finally reached Shankarachala" said the Queen, excitedly.

They dropped the anchor and got off the giant ship where soldiers were already there to escort them into the kingdom.

"Welcome to the Kingdom of Shankarachala Queen Cynthia. The King is waiting for your arrival" said the person leading the soldiers.

They got into the chariots and were heading towards the kingdom. After a while, Queen Cynthia could see big strong gates made out of stone and some gold indulged in it. Connecting to the doors were huge walls protecting the kingdom. They reached the Mian Gate of the Kingdom when suddenly the gates were opened and the King Chakra was waiting on the other side. They got down their chariots and entered the Kingdom.

"Queen Cynthia! My Friend! Welcome to my Kingdom." said King Chakra, holding her right hand and bowing to the Queen.

The Queen, while holding her frock, bowed a little and said, "Long time no see Chakra! I am so happy to be here.

How have you been?"

"I am fine Cynthia. Finally, you remembered your old friend huh? Now let me take you to the castle. People of Shankarachala are waiting for your arrival." said the King while taking her to a huge, heavily decorated elephant.

"King Chakra, don't tell me that I have to ride this elephant now!" said the Queen, confused.

"Don't worry! This is our tradition. This is how we welcome our Guests to the King. It's safe! And if you want, I'll also join you" said the King, assuring the Queen's safety.

The Queen sighed with relief and said "Phew! That would be great then!"

They rode the elephant and entered the Kingdom. The people of Shankarchala welcomed her with the great sounds of *Nadhaswara and shehnai* along with the beats of *Dhol.* There was a rain of petals and the people were cheering them while performing a variety of dances in front of the ride.

The Queen was amazed with the view in front of her eyes and said "I have never seen such an astonishing kingdom overflowing with culture and heritage. It feels like a festival."

They reached the palace's main gate. The gates and the walls were made of stone. The King escorted her into the palace. As the Queen went inside, her eyes were filled with the beauty of the palace. It was completely made out of white marble with a hint of gold in it. It was as huge as the walls that were protecting the kingdom. There were gardens surrounding the palace and the walkway.

The King summoned a couple of Chambermaids and asked them to escort the queen and her soldiers to their rooms along with the luggage. While the maids were helping them, one of the maids was trying to take the ancient maroon box.

"DON'T TOUCH THE BLACK BOX!" screamed the queen with terror in her eyes. "Let me hold it." Added the queen.

"I am sorry Your Highness." Said the maid with a dull face. "Hey, that's fine. Don't worry too much about it" said the queen with a refreshing smile on her face.

"Cynthia, there is a huge banquet in the night on your welcome. Please be ready by that time." said the King. "Sure, will be there" replied the queen. The King threw a huge banquet to the entire kingdom in the welcome of Queen Cynthia. It all felt like a festival.

The next day Queen Cynthia and King Chakra along with the ministers assembled in the throne room. She presented all the gifts to the King and then took the unusual box into her hand not even allowing the servants to touch it. The air around the box was not only pretty cold but also suffocating. Except for her men, no one was able to get near the box.

"I hope you remember this box from yesterday, Chakra." Said the Queen.

"Yes! I do. What's exactly there in that box? Why didn't you let the maid touch it?" asked the King with a lot of curiosity. Questions like these were swirling in his head.

The Queen then replied "This is what we call the **Black Box.** Only me and my men can sustain its power. I will answer all your questions in a while. This is the main reason for my visit. Chakra, we need your help. We are unable to sustain him in this Black Box any longer. He must be exorcised as soon as possible".

The King asked, "So do you mean that there is a Curse in that box?"

"Not any curse Chakra, one of the Strongest Curses I've ever known till today. He is also known as ***The Demon of the***

Cold! Said the Queen Cynthia.

King was surprised. He felt something off since the beginning. He doubted what/who the Curse could be. The King didn't want to believe his intuitions. But sadly, his intuitions were right. He was afraid to even utter the name of the Curse.

"I know what's there in that box. I didn't want to believe my intuition. But we can't change the fact. Ok, I will help you. I will take you to the Guruji. I think only he can help us right now." Said the King.

The Queen was delighted and thanked the King for his generosity. The next day the King, Queen and the strongest guards known in the troop started their journey to the Guruji's Ashram. They reached the Ashram. Right when they were about to enter, an icy breeze came from the box, and the atmosphere became cold as if the box was denying to enter the Ashram. Then suddenly they heard a scream from the Ashram.

"STOP THERE! DON'T SET A FOOT INTO THE ASHRAM. DON'T YOU DARE BRING HIM INTO MY ASHRAM."

It was Guruji who screamed. All of them were astonished. His scream sent chills down to their spin. The Guruji came out of the Ashram.

Guruji said "I know what is there in that box. I know why you are here Queen Cynthia the Empress of Albada. As I heard, the people of Albada are trained to sustain the power emitted by the Black Box which can hold the Curse. It is my first time seeing the box in real. I was always amazed by the technology of Albada. But I never expected the Queen herself to come here to seek help to exorcize a Curse. Of course, you don't have a choice as this is known as one of the Strongest Curses. I think you know what I meant Chakra. Finally, he came to where he belonged."

The Queen was surprised. "That's what I expect from the Great Guruji Suryavasta, the destroyer of the curses." Said the queen.

The Guruji said "I am not the destroyer. I just show them the right way. And that is what exorcism does. Anyways, let me take you to the place, far away from the Kingdom, where we can seal him."

"Seal him? Aren't we going to exorcize him?" asked the Queen, confused.

The Guruji replied "I will explain everything while we are on the way. Chakra, we have to immediately start to the Suddhikarna Kshetra. We have to seal him as soon as possible."

"Queen Cynthia please hand over the box to me" said Guruji.

"It's fine Guruji I can carry it" said the Queen politely.

Guruji replied "You might not be aware but this box is consuming your energy and I can sense that your energy levels have been degraded so much. If it reduces more, then you might even die. Your power will be necessary to protect us in the Kshetra. So, hand over the box to me and take this medicine to regain your energy."

The Queen handed over the box to Guruji. They got into the Chariot and started their journey to the Kshetra. There were three Chariots in total. Two with the Guards, and one with the King, Queen and Guruji.

The Queen asked Guruji "If I am not mistaken, I remember you said we have to seal the Curse. Can you tell me why aren't we exorcizing it?"

Guruji replied "Yes, I did say that we have to Seal the Curse. As you know the Curse in this box is the Demon of Cold. I am quite surprised that Albada was able to build a box that could sustain him for this long time. He might break out any time sooner. There are two ways to Exorcize this Curse. First, we have to seal him and keep him at a safe place for some time till his power is drained to 1/4th of what it is now and throw him into hell. As per my estimation, we have to keep him sealed for almost 500 years."

"500 years!!! What are you saying Guruji?!" said the Queen.

Guruji replied, "He is at his peak right now. The seal is a pretty strong one and will drain his power. We have to make sure that he remains in this seal for 500 years".

"Isn't there any other way Guruji?" asked the Queen.

Guruji replied, "There is another way but it is kind of risky".

"What is that Guruji?" Asked King Chakra.

Guruji replied "For that, we need to let the Curse possess a human body. After the possession, we have to extract the Curse and drench the Curse with the blood of the body it possessed. That will make the Curse weak and we can return him where he belonged. But as I said this is a risky process. There are chances where the curse can become powerful after possessing the human body. But this happens when the curse possesses a compatible body. And considering him we are not in a position to control him. And for this, we have to sacrifice a human as there are only a few people in this whole world who can have him and stay alive and that too for some time. He can't possess a normal human body as they don't have the power to sustain his power. So, to exorcize him we must sacrifice a strong human being which I don't prefer. So, I think it's better if we seal him. The longer we seal him, the weaker he gets, but remember he is still the same, the Demon of the Cold".

"We have arrived Guruji," said the King.

Everybody got down their Chariots and headed towards the Kshetra. The Suddhikarana Kshetra was located on the outskirts of the kingdom, on top of the hill. The Kshetra looked like an abandoned hut. The walls had Matras written on them. It was a one-room hut with a basement door. There was only one big table located in the middle of the room. There was nothing else in the hut except for the table.

Guruji placed the box in the middle of the table and opened it. And there comes the Curse. Opening the Box made some of them faint. Withstanding such a huge energy was getting difficult. Queen Cynthia cast an energy shield which protected everyone and gave them the power to withstand it.

Guruji took a book out of his bag and started to read the Mantras. The Mantras give the Curse a human form which can be easily separated into pieces. The Curse was trying to get down from the table but he couldn't as the table was enchanted. Then Guruji summoned the Mother of Curses, Shrishtara. She was holding the Curse onto the table so that he couldn't move.

As Guruji kept on reading the Mantras, the Curse was getting disintegrated into pieces. The process was so painful that his cry was piercing the ears of everyone. He disintegrated into 13 different pieces. The mother of Curses was sent back. These pieces have been reduced into small chunks and the small strips of paper with Mantras written on them wrapped the chunks.

Now the final step, Guruji extracted some blood from his own body and dipped these chunks in the blood. In the entire Kshetra Guruji was the only one who could withstand the Curse without any support. His blood has the power to negate the energy of the Curse. Guruji placed there

13 Chunks, soaked in his blood, in the box. He wrapped the box with a special cloth which had strong mantras written on it and placed that box and the book in the corner of the room.

"What now Guruji?" asked the Queen.

Guruji replied "This box should be untouched for 500 years. I have cast a mantra which will open The Door of Hell after 500 years and suck this box into itself. That basement door will be the Door of Hell. And King Chakra, announce that this place is forbidden to everyone in this Kingdom. Make sure you keep protection to this place and no one enters this Kshetra. For our further exorcising, I will build another Kshetra. I will also cast a Mantra which prevents people from entering this Kshetra. This Mantra will last for 500 years. I will leave my book and my Rudraksha Maala here."

King Chakra asked, "Guruji, I am asking this out of pure curiosity, what happens if anyone opens this box before 500 years?"

Guruji replied "As per my knowledge no one in this world is in a position to sustain the energy this box emits. So, opening the box is an impossible case. But as time passes the power of the box will be reduced and people might end up opening it. The main problem is not opening the box, the main problem comes when the seal applied to these chunks is removed. When that happens and the chunks are put together, there are high chances that he might return. He might be powerless, but if he possesses a body, that might be an issue."

King Chakra, along with the help of Queen Cynthia started the preparations to seal the Kshetra. This process continued for 15 days.

Finally, the Kshetra sealing has been finished. Queen Cynthia was preparing her return to Albada. But for one last time, she wanted to pay her gratitude to Guruji.

"Thank you so much, Guruji. Now people of Albada can have fearless nights after a long time." Said the Queen with a relief in her face.

Guruji replied "Don't thank me, Thank Lord Shiva. He was the one who brought you to me. I hope Lord Shiva will take care of all of us and prevent XXXX who is also the XXXXXXXX from coming out of that box......"

Whatever Guruji said sounded like a muffled voice. It was like she missed hearing the most important part...

And the dream ends...

-x-x-chapter end-x-x-

II

THE ABANDONED HUT

That was a pretty sunny day. The time was 7.30 in the morning. Everybody was rushing to their workplace or school. It was a busy morning but also a pretty normal one. It was the time when the existence of Curses was a myth. The time when exorcism methods are not even known to people. The time when all the Curses are sleeping and waiting for HIS arrival....

Bhanumathi, a fresher who got placed into a well-known MNC, had to go to the Office. She was struggling to wake up, shivering and flailing her arms and legs. There was a whisper in her ear, a creepy one saying "Find Me!". Then suddenly, she woke up with a huge gasp. "What was this all about?" she murmured. It took her some time to settle down and return to her senses.

Bhanumathi got out the bed and looked at herself in the mirror where she saw the reflection of the wall clock. She realised that she already missed her office bus. She got ready, took her bag and ran. She barely reached the office in time.

"What happened Bhanu you overslept again huh?" giggled Varsha. Varsha was her colleague and also her best friend in the office.

"No Varsha I had a pretty weird dream."

"Again?" asked Varsha.

"No, this time it's somewhat different. But the problem is I don't remember it, again," said Bhanumathi.

"Ok, don't think much about it. We have a lot of tasks pending to do. Let's think about that first" said Varsha and they headed towards their desks.

"By the way where is Adith? Don't tell me he missed the bus again!" said Bhanumathi.

"No, I didn't." said the guy sitting opposite to their cubical. He was Adith, a fresher just like Bhanumathi.

"Oh, I thought you missed the bus again" said Bhanumathi giggling at the same time.

It was lunchtime. The three of them took their plates and sat at the table to dine in. Varsha started the conversation by mentioning the article that she read in the morning while on her way to the office.

"Hey did you guys hear about this Abandoned Hut rumoured to be on top of the Forbidden Hill? People say that they hear weird noises from that hut. Like someone is screaming and asking for help. Reading the article itself gave me chills. What do you guys think?"

"Hey, Varsha. Let me ask you one thing. If that Hill is forbidden, how do you think people managed to go there and find an Abandoned Hut on top of the hill? Did you forget how high the protection is there for the Forbidden Hill? The government says that there is danger in that hill but they never made it clear. No one in this world is allowed to climb that hill. Don't believe in that rubbish. People just write what they want for their sales," said Adith.

Before Varsha could say something, Adith interrupted and said "Okay, now let's have lunch. It's already getting late." They continued to have their lunch and went back to continue their work.

The discussion that happened during lunchtime was not getting off Bhanumathi's head. She felt like she was familiar with that place, the Abandoned Hut and the weird screams. It didn't seem like some mere story to her or some random article, it felt so real like she already experienced it. The whisper that she heard in the morning echoed in her head. The more she thought about all these, the faster her heart raced.

Bhanumathi's curiosity about the Hill and the Hut was overflowing. "Could the dream be linked to that article? Why did *I* get that dream? Could this be some warning or something?" all these questions swirled in her head. She wasn't able to concentrate on the work. She ended up thinking about that the whole day.

"Why do you look so lost today Bhanu?" asked Varsha.

"It's nothing, Varsha, just thinking about something. Anyways see you tomorrow!" said Bhanumathi and headed back to her home.

Bhanumathi couldn't remove the Forbidden Hill from her head. She opened her laptop and started searching for more articles about the Forbidden Hill. The whole night passed by. She didn't realise when she slept. As always, she woke up with her mother's scream. She rushed to the office as she was getting late, again.

"What happened Bhanu? You were never like this. Even today you look so lost. Is there something that has been disturbing you?" asked Varsha out of curiosity.

"The thing is I haven't been able to remove the Forbidden Hill from my head. And yesterday I got a dream where I was in a dark hut and someone was screaming from the corner of the room. I have never seen that hut in my life. I have a hunch that this might be related to that Forbidden Hill and the dream I got the other day." Said Bhanumathi.

"Don't you think you are thinking too much about that hill? There is nothing in that place. These people are creating some drama and injecting it onto your head!" said Adith furiously.

"Oh, so if that's the case then why don't we check it out? Why don't we go there and see if the hut exists or not?" asked Varsha.

"Are you insane! We are talking about Forbidden Hill which is highly secured. How do you think we can even go to its vicinity?" said Adith, furiously.

Varsha stuttered and replied "I-I will think something about it. I know someone who can be of help."

Adith chuckled and said "Hah! In your dreams," and returned to work.

"You see Bhanu, I will get all the information and then I will talk to him," said Varsha before returning to her place.

Bhanumathi couldn't stop them as she was stuck in the thoughts swirling in her head. She knows, that going there is an impossible task but she also wants to gamble on her intuitions by trusting Varsha. She decided that remaining silent was the best thing she could do now.

The next day Varsha came early to the office and asked Bhanumathi and Adith to be there. She was ready with the information and a proper plan to get into the Forbidden Hill. They took a small discussion room and Varsha started to explain the plan.

"The guards only guard the bottom of the hill. There will be no guards on the hill as no one is permitted there. The security is pretty tight. We have only one way to go to the hill. That is when the guards change their shifts. There will be a 2 minutes gap where there won't be a single guard. We need to utilize that time and enter the hill without them knowing. There is no laser protection or any booby traps. That's a plus point for us." Said Varsha.

"How do you know all this Varsha?" asked Bhanumathi.

"One of my uncle's friends used to work as a guard over there." Said Varsha.

"Then how are we going to escape the Cameras? And about the huge wall that is at the bottom of the hill? How are we planning to cross that?" asked Adith.

"Woah! Woah! Relax. I have a plan for that too. There is going to be a power outbreak for 2 hours in that area and that matches the shift time. We can use that as our chance and go. And about the wall, there are small bricks which are popped out of the wall which may work as stairs for us. So, what do you guys say? Will you join us then, Adith?" asked Varsha.

"Okay fine. I will come along with you guys," said Adith. Finally, all three agreed on one point. Bhanumathi was tense as she was getting bad feelings about it. But the cloud of curiosity covered her tension. She wanted to try going there by herself and verify if that was actually connected to her strange dream.

Two days left for the planned day. Bhanumathi convinced her parents to allow her to stay at Varsha's place that night. They went shopping to buy all the necessary items for the trek. They were super excited for the day to come. All the items were kept in Varsha's place. They rehearsed the execution of the plan almost a hundred times.

Bhanumathi's instincts were stopping her from going, but her heart wanted to know the answers. One more day to go. And they were finally ready and excited to go.

The day arrived. They finished their work early that day and headed to Varsha's place. They started packing all the tools, extra pair of clothes, food and first-aid kit and were ready to go. As the hill was in a walkable distance from Varsha's place they started their journey ten minutes before the power outbreak. They reached the hill on time.

It was around 9.45 PM, right after they reached the power outbreak happened. It was a full moon night. The night felt like it had been waiting for this day for a long time. The clouds covered the moon. It was like the clouds were helping them. The guards went on the shift change. Right after the guards left, the three of them ran at a rapid speed and started climbing the wall. They tied the rope to their waists so that if one falls the others can catch them. They didn't look down and climbed the wall.

It was 10.00 PM. On the other side of the wall was a thick dense forest. They climbed down the wall with the help of the bricks. The clouds cleared the path to the moon and the forest looked stunning and spooky in the moonlight. Bhanumathi was feeling a sharp pain in her head.

Bhanumathi could see some flashes in her head which showed her a similar mountain. In the flash, she was in a chariot and going up the hill. She realised that it was from her dream that she had the other day.

When everyone was confused about what to do next, she wanted to trust these flashes and guide her friends. They started their journey to the hill covered with the dense forest. Both Varsha and Adith were amused by the way Bhanumathi was guiding them.

"How do you know the way? This isn't your first time right" asked Varsha curiously.

"No, this is my first time! I don't know what's going on but for now, trust me and follow me," replied Bhanumathi. They didn't utter a word and followed her.

It was the time which made today a past and tomorrow a present. It was the time when people say the Devils wake up from the darkness. They could see the surroundings covered in a bright silver light as the moon looked like a luminous orb casting an eternal brightness. And there they saw an **Abandoned Hut**. The aura around them suddenly became spooky and the hut was making it worse. There was an icy cold breeze coming out of the hut. There was a whisper from the hut saying "Free Me!".

"Did you hear that?" asked Bhanumathi curiously.

"Hear what?" said Adith.

"Didn't you guys hear, the whisper?" replied Bhanumathi with a slight shiver.

"I-I think you are just hearing things," stuttered Varsha.

They felt chills down their spines as they saw the Hut covered with dark green paint and a No Entry sign outside. They can sense that something is trying to pull them inside. The three stood outside the Abandoned hut wondering what to do next.

-x-x-chapter end-x-x-

III

THE BOX

The darkness enveloped the entire place where the only light sources were three flashlights and the Moon. But the moonlight dominated the flashlights. The night was like a Twilight waiting for this moment. The cry of the owls was harmonising with the sound of the breeze.

They finally reached the Hut. The three of them felt discomfort near the hut. Their hands and legs were shivering. Something was stopping them from going any further, but their hearts were curious to find out what was inside.

"W…We saw the hut right l…let's go back now. I…It's already pretty late," said Varsha.

"Yes, you are right, it's better if we go back," added Adith.

But Bhanumathi ignored them and went inside. It was like she didn't even listen to what they said. There was some enthusiasm in her eyes. Those eyes weren't scared. They were looking for answers.

"Come on Bhanu, what are you doing? Let's go back." Said Adith.

Bhanumathi didn't listen to Adith. She went to the door and tried opening it. There were some locks attached to the doors.

"What are you doing Bhanu? Can't you see the doors are locked?" asked Varsha furiously.

To everyone's surprise, the locks fell themselves and the doors opened with a creaky noise.

"We took a lot of risk not just to see the hut and go. Let's see what's inside" said Bhanumathi while heading inside the hut.

As the doors got opened, a cold breeze hit them from inside. Surprisingly, the Hut looked pretty neat inside. It had dark green walls and mantras written on them. They went inside. As they were exploring the place, they found a door leading to the basement, they assumed. None of them dared to go inside.

Varsha and Adith were looking at the mantras painted on the walls and were trying to decipher them. "*Om Dum Durgayei Namaha*" and "*Om Kreem Kalikaye Namaha*" were written on the walls. There was a huge wooden table in the middle of the hut.

Bhanumathi wondered "Why does this place look so similar? Why does it feel like I have been here before? Is it because of the dream?"

She was walking around the table when something strange in the corner of the room caught her attention. It was a box with some cloth wrapped around it. The air around the box was so cold. Along with it, a book and a Rudhraksha maala were also there.

"Guys! Look what at this?" said Bhanumathi pointing towards the box.

"What can this be? Does this box have an antique treasure in it?" wondered Varsha.

"Not sure, maybe. What do you think Bhanu?" asked Adith.

Bhanumathi became silent. She didn't reply to what Adith asked. She was zoned out the whole time. Both Varsha and Adith didn't understand what was going on.

Bhanumathi felt a sharp pain in her head. She was hearing things, whispers. Whispers like "Hurry Up! Free Me!". Bhanumathi's entire body was shivering. The whispers were getting louder. The closer they went to the box, the colder the air became. Irrespective of the cool atmosphere Bhanumathi was sweating. She couldn't take it. She understood that it was not safe to be there.

And then suddenly, "Guys! Let's get the hell out of here. I don't like it in here," said Bhanumathi and ran out of the hut.

"Hey, Bhanu! Stop!" screamed Varsha and Adith while running behind her to stop her.

"What's wrong with her? Why is she acting like that?" Asked Adith to Varsha.

"How would I know?" screamed Varsha while panting.

Varsha and Adith tried to stop her, then she screamed "Trust me and follow me". After a while, Bhanumathi suddenly stopped in the middle of the forest.

"What the hell is wrong with you?" asked Adith.

"Yeah Bhanu, why are you running and why did we stop in the middle of the forest?" added Varsha.

"I know a way to return to City without letting the guards know." Said Bhanumathi.

"What are you talking about? How?" screamed both.

"See there is a wooden trap door here if you look down. This will take us to the bottom of the hill. As per my estimate, we can reach the bottom of the hill in 30 min.," said Bhanumathi.

"Shut it, Bhanu! Come to your senses!" shouted Varsha. "You were running like hell and stopped in the middle of the forest and now you are saying that this is a secret passage to get down the hill? How are you even sure about it?" added Varsha.

"I am sorry for running without giving you guys a reason. The vibe in that hut was becoming worse. It didn't feel safer to stay there any longer. You guys might not believe but all of this seemed so familiar. I can't explain it to you right now but trust me, I will get all of us out of here without risk. And about this secret passage, I know that this will lead us down. I promise I will tell you everything but first let's get out of this hill," said Bhanumathi.

Varsha and Adith agreed with what Bhanumathi said. They decided to put their trust in her. Bhanumathi opened the wooden trap door. It looked like a secret passage made out of wood. Unlike the hut, it was covered with spider webs all around the place. They were getting rid of the webs and walking with their flashlights on. It was so dark inside.

Three of them were scared but they didn't have a choice. Bhanumathi was still getting that weird feeling that she got in the hut. She thought she was getting that feeling because she was still on that hill. She wanted to get out of that place as soon as possible. After almost 35 min of walking, they reached the end of the passage.

Bhanumathi slightly opened the door above her. She could see the road and the guards guarding the fence.

It was around 3.00 AM at midnight. The next guard switch was at 3.05 AM. They waited till the guards left. Suddenly a huge rain started outside. They could hear the thunders. Right when they opened the door a thunderbolt hit the CCTV camera nearby. It was almost like nature was helping them to escape. They took this as a chance and ran.

They reached Varsha's house by 4.00 AM. They were super tired and got into bed as they returned home. The next day, they got ready and headed to the office. They were still tired but they didn't have a choice. They have to act normal so that no one doubts them. Bhanumathi was still getting the same feeling. She didn't understand why.

It was lunchtime. Three of them got their food and took a table. Bhanumathi went to the washroom to wash her hands.

"Guess what I brought." Said Varsha.

"What is it now?" asked Adith.

"You guys won't believe..." by saying Varsha took out a weird-looking box from her bag "Tada!!!" said Varsha after taking it box. It was none other than the same box that they encountered in the hut.

"What is this box doing here? Don't tell me that you brought it!" said Adith.

"Relax Adith. It's not a big deal and stop screaming, everybody is looking at us." Said Varsha.

"Okay fine, now tell me what was the need to bring this box here. Let's keep that aside. Why did you bring that box out of the hut in the first place?" asked Adith.

"Just look at this box! How cool it looks. It has all these mantras written and wrapped around it. Don't you think they did this to hide something valuable? And if it turns out to be something extremely valuable then we can become rich!!!" said Varsha.

"Yeah, you might be correct but..." said Adith with a lot of confusion and doubts.

"There is no but! We are opening it and that's final." Said Varsha.

"Okay fine. But where are we going to open it? I don't think this is the correct place for that. There are people around and they might see us!" asked Adith.

"Hmm, for that, why don't we go to the stairs of the 8ᵗʰ floor of our building? I bet no one would come to that side. After our work, we will go there to open it. And one more thing, let's keep this a secret from Bhanu. We will surprise her." Said Varsha.

"By the way what is taking Bhanu so long?" wondered Adith. By the time he could complete the sentence, Bhanumathi came back.

"Why didn't you guys start your lunch yet?" asked Bhanumathi.

"We were waiting for you to come." Said Varsha.

"Wah! I am delighted. HAHA" giggled Bhanumathi and they continued to have their lunch.

Looks like Varsha and Adith forgot about Bhanumathi's promise, to give them a detailed explanation of her decisions. That was expected as they are up to something new – to find what's in the box.

It was the time between the bright and the dark. The clouds were so desperate to enjoy the twilight that they covered the entire sky. Varsha convinced Bhanumathi to stay back for a bit long after her work. Bhanumathi's manager called her to give her a new task. They took that as a chance and escaped to the 8ᵗʰ floor.

"Are you sure you wanna open it?" asked Adith.

"We came this far now there is no turning back." Replied Varsha.

Bhanumathi finished her meeting and went back to her place. She couldn't find Varsha and Adith at their places. She was about to call Varsha but her eyes caught a strange book in Varsha's bag. She went to the bag and took out the book. That was when she got the answer to the insignificant distress she was facing even after they left the Forbidden

Hill.

Varsha started to take the cloth off that box. It was a thin strip of cloth with mantras written on it. The cloth felt like an infinite strip. After some 5 minutes, they successfully unwrapped it. Both Varsha and Adith were so involved in the unwrapping that they forgot to call Bhanumathi.

Meanwhile, Bhanumathi tried calling both Varsha and Adith but they didn't pick up the call.

"Where are they? I hope they are not up to something stupid. I hope my intuition is wrong" murmured Bhanumathi.

She searched for them all over the campus. She couldn't find them. Bhanumathi suddenly felt chills throughout her body. She could sense that something wrong was going on. Suddenly a place hit her mind. That was the 8th floor. She didn't search the 8th floor yet! She rushed to the 8th floor. She was praying to God for their safety.

In the meantime, Varsha and Adith were ready to open the box. Mother Nature was giving signs that something negative was going to happen. The clouds were rumbling, and the lights were flickering but still. The air became colder even when the Air Conditioners in the building were not working. Bhanumathi was able to sense some danger and she was feeling chills throughout her body.

"Don't you think we have to wait for Bhanu?" asked Adith.

"Nah, it's fine. Anyway, she knows we will be here. By the time she reaches, we will open it and surprise her," said Varsha.

"I still think it's a bad idea." Said Adith.

"Eh, it's fine. I am opening it anyway," said Varsha and opened the box.

Now the box was open. A cold breeze came from inside the box. It gave them chills all over their bodies right away. Bhanumathi was trying to go by lift but none of them were working. So, she took the stairs. At the same time, she was trying to contact them but couldn't reach their numbers. She felt a strong wave of negative energy hitting her. Whispers were revolving in her head – the same ones which she got after the dream and in the Hut.

The inconvenience and the weird feelings were getting stronger and stronger. She got a strong hunch that the box might be there. She was getting some flashes of the dream in which she could hear an old guy speaking about 13 pieces and getting soaked in blood. From those flashes, she could interpret that the box had something sealed and was not supposed to be opened.

Bhanumathi's stress was increasing. She was murmuring "Please don't open the box! Please don't open the box!" repeatedly.

Bhanumathi also understood that she had to return to the hut, where she would find the answers to her distress. As she rushed to the 8th floor, her distress and weird feelings were getting even stronger, making it hard to breathe.

In the meantime, Varsha and Adith saw something in that box. The box had some weird-looking objects with a pretty weird shape. Few are small and few are huge. But all those pieces are wrapped with cloth which looks similar to the one wrapped around the box. But the only difference is these wraps are blood red. Both Varsha and Adith were shocked to see it. Bhanumathi was rushing with her top speed to stop them. She could interpret that something worse is about to happen if they open the box...

-x-x-chapter end-x-x-

IV
THE 13 PIECES

It was around 7.30 PM. There was a huge thunderstorm outside. Everyone in the office left early except for these three. The lights were flickering all over the office, probably because of the transformer blast that happened nearby.

Bhanumathi was rushing to the 8th floor in the stairs. Her distress feeling was getting stronger. She reached till 7th floor and then the pain in her head sharpened. She was getting flashes from her dreams. This time the flashes were so strong that she couldn't even move. The flashes hit her for quite some time.

Finally, Bhanumathi understood what the dream was. She remembered each and everything from that dream. The dream played in her head like a movie – a horror movie. She was so stressed out. She didn't understand what to do. Her whole body was shivering, thinking about the consequences if they did something stupid. All of this made her throat dry and she went to get some water from the pantry.

"Oh my God! I hope they didn't do something stupid. I hope they are safe." Murmured Bhanumathi.

Bhanumathi was in a rush now. She understood the dangers the box can bring once it is opened. The feeling of agony was getting stronger in her. She finally reached the 8th floor.

The place was a total mess. There was a long strip of cloth on the ground and a couple of small red strips near some weird-looking creature crawling on the ground. Some weird-looking objects wrapped around red cloth were lying next to the box. And next to this mess were Adith and Varsha lying down on the stairs, unconscious.

"Oh God, they did it. What the hell is wrong with them? Why did they do such a thing without even uttering a word to me?" thought Bhanumathi. She was furious at first, but then she thought of handling this mess before waking them up.

The amoeba-looking creatures were crawling all over the place. Bhanumathi started to collect them put them in the box and locked it. The Box was shaking and small scream-like sounds were coming out of it. The temperature was freezing. She also kept the red cloth strips in the box and covered the box with the same white strip. She was searching for the Rudraksha mala and found that they both were holding on to it. After clearing the mess, she sprinkled the water on them to wake them up. Sprinkling the water helped them to wake up.

"What's going on here?" asked Varsha with a sleepy voice. Adith was also waking up.

"WHAT THE HELL DID YOU GUYS DO?! DO YOU HAVE ANY IDEA WHAT YOU HAVE DONE?!! HAVE YOU LOST IT? WHO ASKED YOU TO BRING THAT BOX FROM THE HUT AND OPEN IT HERE?!" screamed Bhanumathi out of anger.

"URGHH! Why are you screaming?! Nothing happened right?" said Adith.

"Nothing Happened?! You guys don't know what you have done. You guys have released a CURSE!!!" said Bhanumathi.

"What Curse? What are you talking about? I think you are the one who lost it not us." Giggled Varsha.

"Oh my god, understand the seriousness of the situation!" screamed Bhanumathi.

Bhanumathi took a deep breath. She said "Ok listen, I know you guys won't believe it. But before I say anything, answer to this - Do you remember what happened before you fainted?" asked Bhanumathi.

"We came here and opened that box. After that, I don't remember what happened. How about you Varsha?" asked Adith to Varsha.

"As far as I remember we opened the box and there were some weird objects wrapped with the red cloth. I tried to open one and then.... I don't remember anything after that." Said Varsha.

"Anyways what's the big deal?! I think you are just overthinking. Things like Curses exist in stories, not in the real world. I guess you are watching Anime a lot these days." Added Varsha.

"I know this seems like some joke to you, but I am serious. There is a curse sealed in that box. How do you think I was able to guide you guys to the hut? How do you think I knew about the secret passage? And how do you think I was able to warn you to get out of the Hut? Everything is linked – linked to my dream. Even at the hill, I was getting flashes of the routes. And even now I got some flashes. Flashes where some old guy dressed up like a saint, explaining to me about it." Said Bhanumathi.

"What are you talking about? We are not able to understand. Do you mean you know what's in this box?"

asked Adith.

"Yes, I know what's there in this box. Let me tell you what exactly I dreamed about," said Bhanumathi.

Bhanumathi took them to the pantry and gave them some water to drink. Bhanumathi held onto the box and made sure that none of them were near it. After they got comfortable, she started to tell them about her dream.

"I guess it was the time when King Chakra used to rule. Probably, some 500 years ago. It was a happy kingdom known for its wealth and exorcism methods."

"Exorcism?! What are you talking about?" asked Varsha.

"Yes, Exorcism. I have read about it in some articles and researched it. I found some relics and old texts that explain the exorcism methods just like this book." Said Bhanumathi. She opened the book she was holding onto and showed the pages with weird symbols and some horrifying creatures drawn on them.

"Let me continue my dream. One day a beautiful-looking princess came to our kingdom to meet her old friend King Chakra. Her name was Queen Cynthia from Albada."

"Albada?! The Kingdom that vanished a couple of centuries ago?" asked Adith.

"How do you know about that place?" asked Bhanumathi.

"I was always curious about places like Atlantis, the city submerged in the sea, Bermuda Triangle, which pulls any plane that flies over it into itself, and Albada, the most advanced city in the world that vanished without leaving a trace. As far as I remember, the city vanished around 500 years ago. So that means..."

"Yes Adith, I don't think it's just a normal dream. I don't know why we were chosen to do this task and why only I got this dream. But I believe there is some reason behind all this and I will find the reason." Said Bhanumathi.

"Task? What task?" asked Varsha with a lot of confusion.

"Let me continue the dream then you will understand what we are supposed to do." Said Bhanumathi and continued her dream.

"Queen Cynthia didn't come with empty hands. She brought an uncountable number of gifts and a box" and then Bhanumathi pointed to the box lying on the ground.

"This box is known as The Black Box" added Bhanumathi.

"Queen Cynthia said that a curse was trapped in the box and was one of the strongest curses. Even though Albada was known for its advanced exorcism methods, they couldn't deal with this curse and came to India to seek King Chakra's help. King Chakra understood that the Curse was powerful and he couldn't handle it. So, he took her to a Sage named Suryavasta. He was also known as 'Destroyer of the Curses'."

"Yeah, I heard about Guruji Suryavasta." Said Varsha.

"When I was a kid, my mom told me some stories about him. He was powerful and also strong. People say he went to the Himalayas to meditate but few believe he is still alive." Added Varsha.

"Yeah, he was pretty powerful. He was the one who cast the seal onto the Curse. He sensed the Curse from his Ashram and didn't let the King and Queen Cynthia in. He stopped them and came out to look at the box. He understood how powerful the Curse was. It was so powerful that exorcising it was not an option. That is why they decided to seal it and throw it into the hell."

"Then why didn't they throw it then itself? Why did they keep it instead of throwing it right away?" asked Adith.

"Sealing such a powerful curse will drain their complete energies. And to throw it into hell they have to summon the Door of Hell which will consume even more energy. They will end up dying." Replied Bhanumathi.

"Oh, now it makes sense. Okay, continue." Said Adith.

"For Sealing or Exorcizing the Curse they have to go to a specific place. It was located on the outskirts of the Kingdom. They have reached there in no time. It had mantras written on the walls, a huge table in the middle of the room and a door at the corner which will act as the Door of the Hell. They placed the curse on the table and opened it. Queen Cynthia was guarding them by casting a Shield of positive energy. Using the Mantras, Guruji summoned the Mother of Curses. Guruji gave the curse a human form. The Mother of Curses was holding him onto the table. As Guruji read mantras, the curse was disintegrating into pieces. There were 13 pieces of him in total. After the entire process, the Mother of Curses was sent back and Guruji drew blood out of his own body to drench the pieces in them. This will help the curse to neutralise quickly. The time estimated for his energy to be reduced to $1/4^{th}$ of its actual energy was 500 years. So, they left the box right there along with the box and the Rudraksha mala and left the Kshetra. Guruji asked the King to restrict it forever. Guruji also said some more things which I am not able to recollect. But this is all I can remember from my dream." Said Bhanumathi.

"So, wait! Let me process all of it. From your dream, we can say that this box is a special box made in Albada, or whatever that kingdom is. And that place is the Abandoned Hut from the Forbidden Hill. The 13 pieces in this box are the Sealed pieces of one of the most powerful curses. Am I right Bhanu?" asked Varsha.

"Absolutely. So now our main goal is to summon the Door of the Hell and to throw these pieces into the Hell." Said Bhanumathi.

"Are you sure we can do that?" asked Adith.

"Yes. Now the curse is in the state where we can handle it. Thanks to the Rudhraksha maala, you guys were safe. And I had just some trouble with breathing, nothing more than that. So, we can do it and have to do it as soon as possible." Said Bhanumathi.

The three of them went back home. Bhanumathi decided to hold onto the box, book and Rudhraksha maala. They planned to return to the Forbidden Hill during the next power break which was set to happen the next day.

That night was quiet, just like the silence before a storm. They were nervous but also had an excitement that they were going to perform something incredible. They didn't know that not only them but also something or someone was waiting to see what would happen. They are not aware of the problems that they are about to face.

-x-x-chapter end-x-x-

V

THE MOTHER OF CURSES

Bhanumathi couldn't sleep that night. What happened that day was playing in her head in a loop. She did show a strong side to her friends but was scared deep inside.

"What if I make a mistake?" "What if I can't exorcise the curse properly?" "What if I keep their lives at risk?" are the thoughts eating up her sleep.

Bhanumathi decided to read the book she got from the hut to escape from all those thoughts. The book was in *Devanagari* which made it easy for her to read. While reading, she didn't know when she slipped into a deep sleep.

It was around 7.00 AM. The birds chirping pulled Bhanumathi out of her sleep. The three of them decided to meet at Varsha's place. Bhanumathi took the box, book and Rudhraksha maala and was set to go to Varsha's house. The power break that was about to happen that day in the evening. So, they decided to rehearse what they were supposed to do that day.

The time was around 10.00 AM. They finished their breakfast and rushed to the terrace. Bhanumathi opened the book and started explaining the process.

"Last night I started reading the book so that we can perform this execution without any mistake. From that book I was able to interpret that the Abandoned Hut has a name". "What?! That spooky hut has a name?!" asked Adith.

"HAHA! Yeah, it does. It is known as Shuddikarana Kshetra." Replied Bhanumathi.

"Woah! That does sound like a Sanskrit name," said Varsha.

"What else do you expect? Ok, let me continue. As per what I understood I will tell you the process, listen carefully. Firstly, we need to place the box – with the curse contained in it – on the table. By reading the mantras from this page we can extract that curse and give it a humanoid physical form. After that, we have to summon the Mother of Curses. The Mother of Curses helps in holding the curse while we read the mantras to make the curse weak. When the curse gets weak, we must summon the Door of Hell to send back the curse. The Mother of Curses also returns to Hell along with the Curse." Said Bhanumathi while pointing out the mantras that are supposed to be read while doing the procedure.

Varsha's eyes widened with fear. "Bhanu, d-do you think we can handle this? All of this sounds so dangerous. Why don't we ask someone about it? There would be someone who can guide us" said Varsha with a trembling voice.

"I believe... no I am sure that we can do it. And who can we consult about this? Did you hear any of our parents or grandparents talk about curses or exorcism? I don't think anyone in this world can help us out with it. I even learned about it from a dream. Don't you think all of this means something? From my dream, I understood that this curse must be exorcized after 500 years. And I believe that this is the right time. Don't worry too much about it. We will pull this off perfectly. Trust me." Said Bhanumathi.

It was the time when people got the chance to witness the beautiful twilight, but the clouds wanted it to themselves. The power break was planned to happen in the next 2 hrs. This power break will last for almost 2 hrs., 30 minutes. They packed all the necessary items.

Surprisingly, Bhanumathi was the only one who could hold the box longer without issues. Varsha tried, but it seemed like her energy was sucked by the box making her faint. The same happened with Adith. So, it has been decided that Bhanumathi will hold it for a longer time and if she is tired, she will pass it on to Varsha or Adith.

It's around 7.45 PM, 15 minutes for a Power break. They are already near the hill waiting for the power out-break. Their hearts were racing faster than a bullet train. As they were getting closer, the feeling of fear and anxiety increased. Bhanumathi held the box tight. They decided to use the secret passage rather than climbing that gigantic wall. They were making all the necessary preparations for the trek and suddenly, the power out-break happened. All the CCTVs were turned off due to the outbreak. They took that as a chance and rushed to the Gate of Secret Passage.

The three entered the passage without any issue and reached the Forbidden Hill. As they came out of the passage they could see a dense forest. Nothing had changed since the last time except the brighter moon – shining like a floodlight. The three prayed to God to make everything fine and support them.

It was 9.00 PM by the time they reached the Abandoned Hut.

Bhanumathi pushed the door to open. The creaky noise echoed in the hut. Bats were flying all over the hut as the doors opened. Unlike the last time, this time the hut did look like it was 500 years old. Bhanumathi gave the box to Varsha and asked her to place it on the table, as she was at her limit. She took the Rudhraksha maala from Adith and Chanted 'OM Namah Shivaayah' for 108 times. Surprisingly, that helped her to recharge energy.

Varsha was holding the book to read the mantras out loud. Bhanumathi and Adith stood a bit far and were holding the Rudhraksha maala.

Bhanumathi was getting a Sharp pain in her head. She understood that it was the Flashes, but she wasn't paying attention to them. Bhanumathi came towards the table and opened the Box.

The huge thunderbolt strokes a tree near the hut right after opening the box. The leaves were rumbling and the cries of the bats were getting louder. The Box's negative energy was so powerful that it made Adith faint. Bhanumathi gave the Rudhraksha maala to Varsha and went back to Adith.

Varsha went near the table. She opened the book and with a deep breath, she started to read mantras. While she was reading, the cloth on the pieces unwrapped by itself. Beneath the cloth were some weird-shaped objects. They were floating in the air. As the mantras continued, the pieces joined to one another creating a huge Blood Red coloured ball that was taking a humanoid shape. As it was taking Humanoid form, the energy emitted by the curse was so extreme that it was becoming difficult for them to even stand.

At that time, out of nowhere, there was a Shield over them that was protecting them and giving them energy.

When Varsha turned back to look from where this shield was coming, she noticed that Bhanumathi was casting the Shield.

"How are you able to do that?!" asked Varsha.

"I don't know!!! First, continue with the mantras and give the Rudhraksha maala to Adith. And Adith, you hold my arm with the maala. It will help us recharge. I will protect you guys no matter what." Said Bhanumathi.

Varsha continued to read Mantras. The sharp pain in Bhanumathi's head was increasing which she couldn't control. Varsha summoned The Mother of Curses, as the Curse took complete humanoid form.

The Sky was roaring. There was a horrible thunderstorm outside. The Mother of Curses was struggling to hold the Curse onto the table. The Mantras that Varsha was chanting were not having any effect. The environment turned into chaos.

Varsha was screaming "THESE MANTRAS ARE NOT HAVING ANY EFFECT!!! WHAT SHOULD WE DO NOW BHANU!!!".

"Wait! Let me think! Even I am not sure what the hell is going on HERE!!!" said Bhanumathi.

The cry of both Mother of Curses and the Curse was piercing their ears. The floor was shaking, the Storm was increasing, and their screams were becoming louder and louder. Bhanumathi's Headache was also increasing.

Suddenly, they heard a scream which almost exploded their earbuds. That scream came from the table. At the same time, the Flashes captured Bhanumathi.

It was a scene linked to that dream, a scene from 500 years ago. She could hear an old man speaking. She realized that it was none other than Guruji. Guruji was discussing something about the curse with King Chakra and Queen

Cynthia.

Guruji said *"Don't thank me. Thank Lord Shiva.* Make sure that the curse is preserved in that box. Don't let even a single human near this hill. After 500 years this curse must be sent back no matter what. He is one of the most powerful curses. Even The Mother of Curses struggled to control him. After 500 years we must throw the box into hell *as it is.* He should not take the humanoid form. The human form makes it easy for him to gain his energy back and possess a body. If that happens then there will be no stopping for his actions. And the history will repeat..."

Bhanumathi came back to her consciousness by the screams of Varsha and Adith. She heard a voice like a whisper saying "Hah! Finally, I am Free!" By the time she could comprehend what was going on, Varsha and Adith left the hut and closed the door. She turned toward the table and the thing she saw made her entire body freeze.

The Mother of Curses was lying dead on the table and the curse was looking at her with the creepiest smile. He was very tall with long sticklike hands and legs with dark blood-red skin. The rumbling clouds declared the arrival of something demonic, something evil. It felt like there was a lot of negative energy in the air – no – the negative forces which were hidden till today were coming back.

Bhanumathi's heart was beating so loud that she could hear her heartbeat. Her entire body was shivering non-stop just by looking at the creepy smile of the dark thing standing near the table. At that time what Guruji said in that dream came to her mind. The muffled statement during the end of the dream was clearer now.

"I hope Lord Shiva will take care of all of us and prevent **SHISHIRA** *who is also the* **King of CURSES** *from coming out of the box......"*

At that time only one thing was running in her mind –
"What have I done?"

Now the story Begins.
End of Part 1

A Fiction by Ashira